Katie and the Smallest Bear

Katie and
the Smallest Bear

Story by
Ruth McCarthy

Pictures by
Emilie Boon

Alfred A. Knopf · New York

For Steven

This is a Borzoi Book published by Alfred A. Knopf, Inc.
Text copyright © 1985 by Ruth McCarthy
Illustrations copyright © 1985 by Emilie Boon
All rights reserved under International and Pan-American
Copyright Conventions. Published in the United States by Alfred A. Knopf, Inc.,.
New York. Distributed by Random House, Inc., New York.
First published in Great Britain by William Heinemann, Ltd., London.
Manufactured in Italy   10 9 8 7 6 5 4 3 2 1
First American Edition

Library of Congress Cataloging in Publication Data
McCarthy, Ruth. Katie and the smallest bear.
Summary: Katie and the smallest bear from the zoo
enjoy an afternoon of fun on the playground and
afterwards have a lovely snack. [1. Bears—Fiction.
2. Play—Fiction] I. Boon, Emilie, ill.   II. Title.
PZ7.M478413Kat 1985 [E] 85-9791
ISBN 0-394-87855-8   ISBN 0-394-97855-2 (lib. bdg.)

The smallest bear was lonely. It was a
lovely sunny day and he had nobody
to play with.

Then he saw a little girl looking through
the fence at him.

"Hello," she said. "I'm Katie. Will you come and play?"

"Oh, yes!" said the smallest bear. "I'll come now!"

So he wriggled under the fence to her.
Katie gave him her hat and scarf to wear,

so he looked just like a fat little boy
in a fur coat, and they walked
out of the zoo,
along the road,
and into the park.

They ran past the ducks,
chased two squirrels up a tree,
and rushed into the playground.

There was a swing, a seesaw, a slide, and a roundabout.

The smallest bear pushed Katie on the swing—higher and higher and higher—as high as the sky.

Then they went on the seesaw. Up, down, up, down, UP!

Katie went on the slide first. The smallest bear whizzed down behind her— his slippery fur made him very fast—and he went BUMP at the bottom.

They went on the roundabout together, whirling 'round and 'round until Katie felt dizzy and the smallest bear's hat flew off.

They played and played and played until Katie said, "I'm hungry. Let's go home for lunch."

So they went home to Katie's house, where they had sticky honey sandwiches, bananas and yogurt, and big glasses of orange juice.

"I want to go home now," said the smallest bear when he'd finished his lunch.

"All right," said Katie, "I'll take you."
So they walked
out of the house,
along the road,
and back to the zoo.

"Good-bye," said the smallest bear. "Can we play another day?"

"Good-bye," said Katie. "We'll go to the park again soon." And they did.

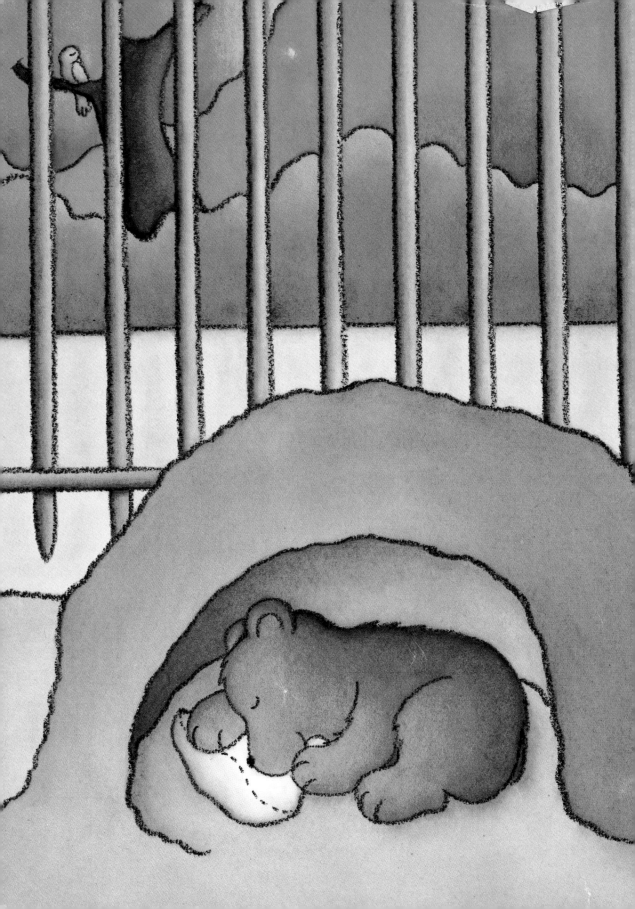